Verses for Young Readers
by David McCord

FAR AND FEW
TAKE SKY
ALL DAY LONG

All Day Long

all day long

long

Fifty Rhymes of the Never Was and Always Is

David McCord

DRAWINGS BY HENRY B. KANE

*Whatever, then, the journey may be, the wayfarer
must bring to it at least as much as it offers.*

Walter de la Mare

Little, Brown & Company   *Boston   Toronto*

LIBRARY OF CONGRESS CATALOG CARD NO. 66-17688

Sixth Printing

Certain of these poems have already appeared in print. I have to thank the editors of the *Atlantic, Harper's,* the *Horn Book,* the *Saturday Review, Boston* magazine, the Boston *Globe,* and the New York *Times Book Review.* "The Tree" (with an illustration by Chiang Yee) was printed as a Christmas poem by Harold Hugo and the Meriden Gravure Company in 1965.

Published simultaneously in Canada
by Little, Brown & Company (Canada) Limited

To
L. Edna Amos
of Portland, Oregon
for all my teachers at
Lincoln High School

Contents

All Day Long

Beneath the pine tree where I sat
to hear what I was looking at,

then by the sounding shore to find
some things the tide had left behind,

I thought about the hilltop blown
upon by all the winds I've known.

Why ask for any better song
in all the wide world all day long?

All Day Long

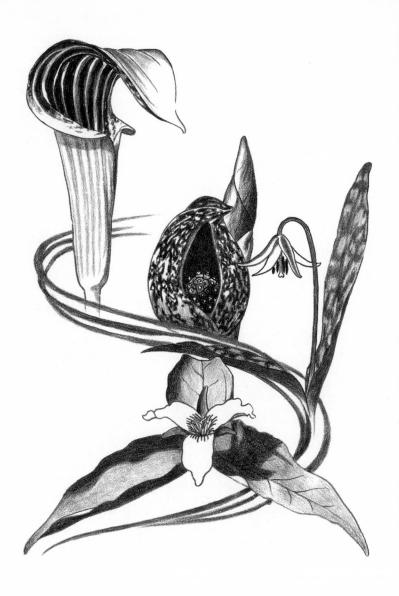

Spring Talk

Jack-in-the-pulpit: Where are you, Jack?
"He's out for a minute; he'll be right back."
Did you hear that? Real pulpit talk:
You hear it only the first spring walk.

Hello, skunk cabbage! Where's old skunk?
"He's rolled up here in the upper bunk."
Of course he isn't — he can't be. Who
Ever heard of a cabbage with bunks for two?

Well, dogtooth violet, and how's that tooth?
"It aches a bit, to tell the truth."
Now you heard *that:* he says it aches.
Let's ask wake-robin when robin wakes,

And toadstools where the toads have gone.
"They all went home. They leave at dawn.
Wake robin, though, and hear him sing."
Who wants to walk with me next spring?

Pad and Pencil

I drew a rabbit. John erased him
and not the dog I said had chased him.

I drew a bear on another page,
but John said, "Put him in a cage."

I drew some mice. John drew the cat
with nasty claws. The mice saw that.

I got them off the page real fast:
the things I draw don't *ever* last.

We drew a bird with one big wing:
he couldn't fly worth anything,

but sat there crumpled on a limb.
John's pencil did a job on *him*.

Three bats were next. I made them fly.
John smudged one out against the sky

above an owl he said could hoot.
He helped me with my wolf. The brute

had lots too long a tail, but we
concealed it all behind a tree.

By then I couldn't think of much
except to draw a rabbit hutch;

but since we had no rabbit now
I drew what must have been a cow,

with curvy horns stuck through the slats —
they both looked something like the bats.

And feeling sad about the bear
inside his cage, I saw just where

I'd draw the door to let him out.
And that's just all of it, about.

Innuendo

You are French? *Je suis.*
You speak French? *Mais oui.*
I don't speak French. *Non?*
I speak English. *Bon!*

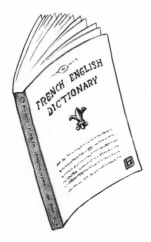

When Monkeys Eat Bananas

When monkeys eat bananas, these
Are monkeys in the zoos or zees.
We get these things all jungled up,
The way chicks have the pip or pup.
For monkeys swinging twos by twos
In threetops not in zees or zoos
Don't have bananas bad for teeth,
But luts of nots below beneath.

Mobile

Our little mobile hangs and swings
And likes a draft and drafty things:

Half-open doors; wide-window breeze,
All people when they cough or sneeze;

Hot dishes giving off their heat;
Big barking dogs, small running feet.

Our mobile's red and made to look
Like fish about to bite a hook:

Six fishes with a hook in front
Of each. They range in size — the runt,

Or baby, up to papa fish,
With hooks to match and make them wish

That they could reach the nice blue worms
A-dangle there with swirly squirms;

Six fishy mouths all open wide,
Six sets of teeth all sharp inside,

Six fishy holes where eyes should be,
Six fish to swim an airy sea.

I'm eating breakfast now, and they
Are watching me. And I must say

That every time I take a bite
I see and feel their sorry plight.

The Clouds

All my life, I guess, I've loved the clouds.
I know some people as I don't know crowds.

Crowds swallow me. I lose myself and feel
that I am someone else, or else not real.

But clouds are not like people: as they pass,
I can know two or three, or such a mass

of flying clouds as fill the summer sky
and lose themselves; for always sailing by

are others just as good, and much the same
for being different. Clouds are like a game

that I don't seem to have to understand,
played without rules, with no one in command;

or like a picture puzzle on the go,
not asking to be solved by me below.

Clouds comfort me, and in such endless grace
I'm never lost and never lose my place.

The cool grey clouds at dawn devise the sea
in perfect stillness: just the beach and me.

Those thunderheads that pile above the sun,
so white before they blacken and I run,

are more than castles, mountains, what you will —
they're all my windows opening, opening still.

The farmer's and the seaman's clouds are plain
bone mackerels that swim before the rain.

I like them just because they serve to warn,
as when in fog the fogman blows his horn;

so puffy clouds that underlie one dread
dark canvas mean a hurricane ahead.

I like slow clouds that slide across the moon:
the long black arrows aimed to reach there soon.

The northern sky: St. Lawrence, the Great Lakes,
is where the west wind over water shakes

the sails of cloudy clipper ships that fill
with cumulus my skylight sill to sill.

All sunset clouds have color and that's when
I look for shape: a shark, a dragon's den,

a spouting whale, a giant, some great bird
or animal of which I've never heard.

I favor clouds that bring a solid fall
of fat wet Christmas flakes of snow; and all

the shower clouds of April come and gone;
big clouds that drag their shadows on the lawn,

or sweep their shadows from the mountain face —
all clouds, all seasons, sizes, any place.

Ten Twice

I say to you just so:
I know you think I think I know I know.
You say to me and I let it sink:
You know I think you think I think you think.

Bridges

The little bridge goes hop-across,
The big one humps his back;
The long one's half a spider web,
The flat one has a track.

The little bridge says, "See my fish";
The big one, "See my river";
The long one says, "See *me!* See *me!*"
The flat one starts to quiver

As you would, too, beneath a train.
The drawbridge says, "Well, I
Am going up for one good squint
About me in the sky."

I know them all: the long one scares,
The drawbridge makes you wait;
The big one dizzies me; I like
The flat one for the freight

That rumbles all its hundred cars
And heads for somewhere west;
But when I'm in the country . . .
Yes, I guess I know you've guessed:

That little bridge of hop-across
Keeps after me to stop.
I watch the wavy fish and see
My face, and maybe drop

A pebble in, or throw a small
Red berry down just right
To float above his fish; he
Doesn't say his fish will bite.

Rapid Reading

"A course in Rabbit Reading?"

"That's what she said. And something else like 'Addled Education.' "

"Rabbits? They can't read. You *know* they can't."

"The one in *Alice* could. At least he had a watch and told the time. And on the front door of his little house — remember? — there was a bright brass plate with W. RAB-BIT on it. I guess he could read *that*. Perhaps he couldn't spell out WHITE. Which shows . . ."

"*Alice* is a book. Look: Rabbits just don't read. They *breed*. She must have said 'Of course, in rabbit breeding . . .' "

"She didn't, though. She said *a* course in *Rabbit Reading*. Why? We haven't any rabbits that I know of."

"You should have asked her."

"She was on the phone with Mrs. Marples. She's still there on the phone with Mrs. Marples. I also heard her say 'Well lettuce, by all means.' What's *addled* anyway?"

"Just nuts, you nut. But *lettuce?* Did she laugh?"

"No."

"Gee, that's funny."

Flicker

Up the road ahead
Flick goes a flicker;
Where the eye is quick
The bird is quicker.
Let the day hold still
So in his haste I hear
wick-whickering of wings
To please my ear.
Above his target tail
A white spot till he's gone
leaves but the chalk-like trail
To follow on
With eye if not with feet.
One feather of his
Floats down. How neat
And yellow it is.

Lemonade

It's lemonading time again:
Some take it sugary, some plain.
"Some take it the way I make it." Jane
Says that, and surely Jane should know,
For though it's noon and business slow,

She tends her shady roadside stand,
Both Greg and John prepared to hand
Each customer a cloudy glass
Of what might almost nearly pass
For lemonade. "Five cents a peg,
Or two for ten. I've change," says Greg:
Five nickels from his piggy-bank,
A dime from each for what they drank
Themselves before they opened shop
And watered down the pitchered pop.

October Wind

There is a sudden little wind that grieves
along the grounded edge of autumn leaves;

there is one even suddener that spreads
a lace of leaves on lawn and flower beds;

and there's a third not ever known to tire
of whirling piled-up leaves in flameless fire

the day before real burning can begin.
If someone says "Go back and rake them in,"

all through the gathered gold you'll hear that sad
small sudden wind just asking why you had

to make such piles unless it was for play.
And is that why you jumped in them today?

Frog in a Bog

Log, bog, and frog
All go together.
The *clementest* weather
(You guessed: the *best*)
For any frog isn't fog.
Give him hot bright sun —
A June one, an August one,
Or any of July's.
Flies are his prize:
Any kind, any size.
He is all eyes for flies.
A frog'll boggle
Up through scud of mud
So he can goggle
From the sedgy edge
Of grasses; or surprise,
Out of delicious skies,
Such wayward wings
Of things that may be had
Just as they tilt and skim
The dry green rim
Of lily pad.

Frog's a queer bloke
To hear him croak;
Queerer still in looks;
Queer leaper into brooks
Or ponds. We swim
Like him, not like a fish,
For he's our dish.
Real frogmen ape his style —
Though we don't see *them* smile.
His wide lips thin
Along his wider grin,
Dive in,
they seem to say,
OK,
Dive in.

Says Tom to Me

Says Tom to me: "I slept the sleep of the just."
"An unjust thing *that* is for a boy like you!
You must have sleep — of course you *must*.
But without it, what did the just man do?"

The Walnut Tree

There was once a swing in a walnut tree,
As tall as double a swing might be,
At the edge of the hill where the branches spread
So it swung the valley right under me;
Then down and back as the valley fled.
I wonder if that old tree is dead?

I could look straight up in the lifting heart
Of the black old walnut there and start
My flying journey from green to blue
With a wish and a half that the ropes would part
And sail me out on a course as true
As the crows in a flock had dared me to.

I swung from the past to the far dim days
Forever ahead of me. Through the haze
I saw the steeple, a flash of white,
And I gave it a shout for the scare and praise
Of being a boy on the verge of flight.
And I pumped on the swing with all my might

Till the valley widened. Oh, I could guess
From the backward No to the forward Yes
That the world begins in the sweep of eye,
With the wonder of all of it more or less
In the last hello and the first goodbye.
And a swing in the walnut tree is why.

Mr. Spade and Mr. Pail

Mr. Spade and Mr. Pail and Mr. Henry Digger,
The three of them, the beach and sun,
The big world growing bigger

As Mr. Spade in Henry's hands
Selects the special kind of sands
That Mr. Pail is made to hold:
Not creamy white or golden gold,
But something super which the sea
Has left for Mr. Henry D.
With which to have his fun.

Now Mr. Pail is fairly full, and Mr. Henry Digger
Has said to Mr. Spade, "I wish
That Mr. Pail were bigger."
But Mr. Pail has just replied
That he is big enough inside;
For after all, when one is filled
And hopping hops, if sand is spilled,
Why then it's up to Mr. Spade
To fix the mess the sand has made.
"But if you catch a fish,"

Says Mr. Spade to Mr. Pail and Mr. Henry Digger,
"You'll need some water. Sand won't do,
And though I might be bigger,
No water ever sticks to *me* —
Not all the water in the sea.
You'd better have me dig a hole,
Then dig a ditch. The sea will roll
Right in, all frothy at the lip,
And Mr. Pail won't mind the dip;
The fish will like it too."

Now Mr. Spade and Mr. Pail — *not* Mr. Henry Digger —
The twain of them are lying where
The sea is growing bigger.
The tide is coming in quite fast,
But Mr. Digger couldn't last
At digging. He has gone to help
Himself to strings of stranded kelp;
So Mr. Pail and Mr. Spade
Are done for if he doesn't wade.
Does no one really care

For Mr. Spade and Mr. Pail? Not even Mr. Digger
Has seen them floating out and how

The waves are breaking bigger,
While Mr. Spade in Mr. Pail
Is saying "Have you hoisted sail?"
And Mr. Pail is saying "No.
I guess perhaps we'd better, though."
But Mr. Spade replies "I think
It might be wiser just to sink;
In fact, we're sinking now."

Oh, Mr. Spade! Oh, Mr. Pail! remember Mr. Digger
While you are restive in your grave —
A grave that's growing bigger.
But don't forget as tides run out
How very soon they turn about.
Yes, you will find yourselves once more,
I'm glad to tell you, on the shore.
"I hear a voice," says Mr. Pail;
"A fish, perhaps, or else a whale;
Or could it be our brave

Young lad — where *are* you, Mr. Spade? — our
      brave young Henry Digger?"
It couldn't, I regret to say;

It might, if he were bigger.
The morrow morning on the beach,
Half buried in the sandy reach,
Lies Mr. Pail with battered face.
Of Mr. Spade not any trace
Until a bather, crying "Oh!"
Has stepped on what I guess you know . . .
Where's Henry, anyway?

Pumpkins

October sun for miles and miles and miles;
and we were passing piles and piles and piles
of pumpkins — pumpkin-like, so like each other
no pumpkin knew one pumpkin from his brother.
If they were carved and placed in aisles and aisles,
with piles and piles of smiles and smiles and smiles
for miles and miles and miles on some dark night,
and one could handle, candle them, and light
the whole creation with Jack Pumpkinheads,
they'd be no wiser. What a pumpkin dreads
is being so conspicuous with eyes
and nose and mouth. Much better off in pies,
say pumpkins. So for miles and miles and miles,
with piles of pumpkins — aisles and aisles of piles —
just putting all their pumpkinheads together,
you couldn't tell what they were thinking: whether
they thought of Halloween, or where they grew
in yellow pumpkin fields. I'd say the view
was pleasing to those pumpkins at the top —
which were of course the best ones in the crop.
But since they had no eyes nowise to know,
they might as well have been down there below;
nor could they guess that mile on mile on mile
some boy was hoping he might see one smile.

Figures of Speech

"Now come to think of it," you say.
I'll come, of course. Come where?

"High time you're up!" *High* time? How high?
Both clock-hands in the air?

You had "a high old time"? I'm glad.
Why *old*, though? Weren't you there?

The Cellar Hole

Between our house and Jack's next door
They dug a cellar long before

Bulldozers were invented. Men
Used picks and spades and dug, and when

They'd dug a big hole three or two
Feet deep that Friday, they were through

Till Monday. Friday night the rain
Came down all night, and it was plain

Not Saturday would stop it, nor
Would Sunday, when it rained some more.

On Monday noon it stopped while we
Were both in school; but after three,

When Jack and I ran home, we found
A pond with no one else around,

And got our rubber boots and stuff.
The month was May, and warm enough.

Jack's steamboat took a while to heat
The boiler, but I had a fleet

Of sailboats going, and my sub
I'd got for Christmas. In the tub

It wasn't much, but now it dived
Right down. Then other kids arrived

With boots and boats and stuff and made
An awful splash. They couldn't wade

Unless they yelled. Their yells were loud,
And pretty soon we had a crowd

Of kids with boots, young brats with boats.
"If we could make a raft that floats,"

Said Johnny, and I said, "Why not
With these three planks?" We sank a lot

Of kids whose boats wound up with keys,
And they wound up by losing these.

Jack had his steamboat going now;
But just as he was showing how

To set the rudder, something broke,
And someone gave the thing a poke,

So round it circled, tooting toots
Just as I filled my rubber boots

With fresh mud-water; but by then
They didn't need it. That was when

Poor Jerry came. He had no luck.
He had no boat. He brought a duck.

A lot of good that did for him:
It didn't want to stay and swim.

Next day they spaded up my sub.
It never worked well in the tub.

Boo Moo

Cats and owls
see better than fowls?
Ducks and pigs
sing better in wigs?
One is false, one partly true.
Perhaps you think the cow says *Moo?*
In Webster's Dictionary, *Boo!*
Just look it up: I ask you to.
Then ask the cow, and I am through.

I'm pretty well, myself. How you?

Young Sammy

Young Sammy, when he was no more
than — maybe less than — yes, than four,
had trouble with the names of things
that walk or swim or fly with wings.
He'd never tell you those are cows.
"See, Sammy? What are those?" "Those clows,"
he'd answer. Chickens in their coop
looked more like jiggins. He would whoop
delight to see a flock of birds,
or — if you understood him — virds.
A turtle, sunning on a log,
to him was turkle; and a frog
became a flog when Sammy spoke
about him. Why not? Flogs can cloak
as frogs cannot; and so his vat
vlew vaster than a tumbly bat.
His rabbits weren't, his labbits were;
his clitten, like the clat, had vur;
the pond was full of pickerel —
too long a word; particural
when there were frogs in it, and tads —

he said that right — and lilyplads
above which sailed the waggonvlies
like whirlybirds cut down to size.
But Sammy now is six and knows
a flog's a frog. If "What are those?"
he says to *you*, your zoo reply
is pachyderms or platypi.

Bumblebee

The bumblebee is bumbly,
acting anything but humbly.
Into flowers he's a tumbler
all day long — a bandit bumbler.
Does his buzzing mean *Beg pardon!*
as he zooms about the garden?
No. And so, if you were roses,
would you want him rubbing noses?
And about that drop of honey:
would *you* sell it for no money?
No again. But bee's to blossom
what persimmon is to possum.

Bumblebee, with yellow sweater,
though you haven't won your letter,
I can see your legs all chappy
like a cowboy's. You're not happy
like a cowboy. No, sir, stranger!
And you pack a lot more danger.
You don't ride the range just singing.
You've got wings. When they're not winging,

I observe that you don't fold 'em.
Honey bees do that. You hold 'em
up. Hold up your flowers, too;
but please don't ever . . .

> you know who!

OZ

Is Oz?
Oz was.
I knew it well.
Is Oz?
Dear Land! It cast a spell
on me that I'm not over yet.
Can you imagine I'd forget
the Wizard? Could my mind erase
Tin Woodman, Dorothy? Misplace
Jack Pumpkinhead, the Scarecrow, Tip?
The Saw-Horse, Gump, Billina? Skip
the Cowardly Lion? I guess not!
Would Tiktok tick if one forgot
the Nome King? What would Scarecrow do
to me if I'd not tell you who
was H. M. Woggle-Bug, T.E.?
His letters still spell THEM to me.
THEM isn't all that they imply:
H.M.T.E. *is* THEM, though. Try
H(2) M(4) T(1) and E,
you'll find, just must be — oh, yes, (3).

43

And then there's Ozma who, of course,
was — that's a secret. Funny! Force
of habit makes me say these things.
The Wheelers? Did they fly with wings?
They rolled on wheels. The Scoodlers? Should
I blurt out *everything?* I could.
This Ozman (which I am) still keeps

his hat on even while he sleeps,
for who can say in Oz what's next?
It doesn't do to tax the text.
Just keep on going, book through book:
In Oz you see before you look.
In Oz you wake before you dream,
in Oz you're never what you seem,
in Oz you do before you dare.
In Oz — but maybe you've been there?
A lot of people have, I guess.
Is Oz then? Yes, yes, three times yes!
Is Oz?

You *know* it is, don't you?
I hoped you did.
I thought you do.

Corinna

Dinner!
Where's Corinna?
Dinner!
Where's Corinner?
Where's Corinner? Innerout?
Corinner risout, no doubt.
Corinner! *Dinner!*
Hearer shout?
And now Corinner resin
from wherever Corinner rasbin.
Corinner reatser dinner
at last — and fast:
most of it sinner.

Ants and Sailboats

I ate my sandwich on the rocks.
The racing boats were out at sea,
All white and misty, and the docks
Across the harbor looked at me.

An ant came by. I scattered crumbs,
Some big ones, mostly from the crust.
The sails stuck up like tiny thumbs
And fingernails. I guess I must

Have watched ten minutes while they spread
Or stacked themselves like cards to bunch
Beyond the islands; and I fed
Myself the peach and finished lunch.

From time to time I watched the ant:
He circled round as he'd refuse
One crumb and then another. Can't
Make up his mind which one to choose,

I thought; and then a bigger red
And bully ant came up and they
Compared antennae. Which one fled?
The red one. When he ran away

Some other black ones zagged across
The rock face. Each one seemed to know
The others, but if one was boss,
I couldn't tell. The sails stood low

Against the sky; but ants move fast.
And pretty soon one got his nips
On such a crumb as made a vast
Unwieldy burden. All the ships

And sails out quartered on the breeze
Were nothing to this active race
Of people shouldering with ease
Their weight, and then some, over space

Of rock and making off for where
They had their crevice home. It could
Have been a long way. Time to spare
Was not for them. This ant was good

At pushing his selection straight
Ahead of him until he came
To obstacles — though not so great
He couldn't pull it over. Game

And solid efforts dragged it up
Each thimble mountain, over straws
Like logs to him, till in the cup
Of one green leaf he seemed to pause,

Then left the crumb and ran for help
Or haven. Fringy grass hung down
Above the rocks where withered kelp
Concealed his passage home to town.

Would he remember where he hid
His food? I looked my last on sails.
Or was it that he never did
Admit himself an ant who fails?

Ptarmigan

O Ptarmigan, O ptarmigan,
O ptarmigan: pt
is such a funny way to start

a name. Don't you agree?
You've never had pneumonia,
though you live among the Lapps
and Eskimos inhabiting
those ice-cold ptops of maps.
There's no one here to ptell me
how you ptolerate that name!
It saddens me to think that
someone like me was to blame.
Some ancient Gael? It wasn't. No,
his word was *tārmachan.*
The Greek for feather? *pteron;* but
did Greeks know how you fan
your feathered feet to walk on snow?
You wouldn't walk on ptar;
and, anyway, the Greeks live south
and never got that far.
Some day, I guess, I'll travel north
and ask a caribou
or reindeer: How's your pterritory?
Got a Pt-V ptoo?

Four Little Ducks

One little duck
In a pond is ducky:
A duck with luck.
Then lucky lucky

Two little ducks
And the pond grows duckier;
Three little ducks
And the ducks' luck luckier.

Four little ducks
Set the big geese hissing.
The old hen clucks
"Four ducks are missing!"

"Four little ducklings,"
Geese tell gander.
Curious clucklings:
Old hen *and* her

Chicks (cheep cheep)
Begin to chorus,
"Ducks! (peep peep)
In the pond before us."

The ducklings quack
Quacks high and thready:
"We won't come back
Until we're ready."

"And when will *that* be?
When? O *when?*"
"O geese O gee!
O when O hen!"

"Fresh young quackers,
Don't you think?"
"Wisecrack crackers!
Let them sink."

The geese hiss hisses,
Hen clucks clucks
With hits and misses
At those young ducks.

55

The ducklings quack quack
Back: "Don't meddle!"
They jibe and tack
(They really pedal);

The quacklings duck
(They're upside down);
Perhaps they're stuck,
Perhaps they'll drown;

Perhaps they'll not,
Perhaps they won't;
They know a lot.
Don't think they don't.

Four little webby
Pinkfoot truants;
It's just well mebbe
They lack influence

And don't know how
Much risk is risky.
A turtle, now,
Could snap one frisky

Foolish swimmer.
They have no mom.
Their chance grows dimmer
As they grow calm.

A turtle big
And round and flat?
The ducks don't dig
A thing like that.

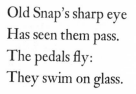

A shadow glides
Up from the mud
Toward undersides
Of flesh and blood.

Old Snap's sharp eye
Has seen them pass.
The pedals fly:
They swim on glass.

Which yellow sailor
Will turtle take?
The geese grow paler,
The chicks all shake.

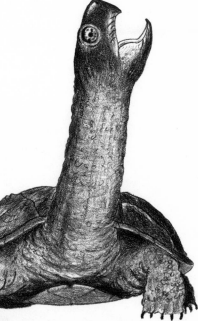

"Look out! Look *out!*"
The geese give warning.
But geese can't shout.
Well, just this morning,

To round them up
Is a boy out rowing.
His dog's no pup:
A wise old knowing

Red retriever,
Name of Thor,
A firm believer
In ducks ashore.

His mouth drools drooly,
Soft and quick;
He does things coolly,
Knows each trick

And duckly skitter:
All old hat
To Thor, more fitter
Than any cat.

He's poised and ready
With big-dog splash!
He's swimming steady
While ducklings dash,

Till one gets caught
And two get caughter,
As three well ought
And four well oughter.

One says, "Yes,"
The second, "Yessir!"
The pond grows less
And less and lesser

Full of flighty
Ducklings. Thor
Gives one good mighty
Shake, once more

Inside the boat.
The big drops shaken
From his red coat,
The unforsaken

Fluffy clutch
Of ducks together
Quack — as much
To say "What weather!"

Geese stop hissing,
Hen-clucks cease.
There's not one missing.
All is peace.

In pondy muck
For Snap no dinner.
No duck, no luck;
He's thin, he's thinner.

The days go by.
No duck appears.
Why magnify
My lack of tears?

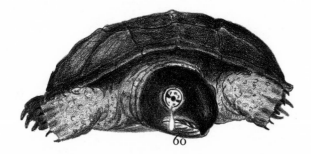

Two Times Three

In summer these —
they always come in threes:
    a spot of hot,
    a pool of cool,
        or else the breeze,
        not round my knees
but up the valley
        soft and light and high
        as bees in trees.

In winter those
three best for when it snows:
    desire of fire,
    of bed ahead —
        no frozen toes,
        dire nosey blows
while up the chimney
        soft and light and high
        smoke cozy goes.

Beech

I like the circling proud old family beech,
The carefully tailored cut of his grey bark;
His lower branches glad enough to reach
Straight out and touch the earth and leave no mark
Against the sky; the way his twigs turn up,
Like fingers of the hand, each barbel cup
Of gold from which will come the bronzy leaf.
His sails and topsails set without a reef,
All summer now he sways across the lawn;
And when from other trees the leaves are gone,
He furls the faded paper his became.
Some flutter dryly mentioning his name,
If you should find them there when only snow
Is on the ground where most leaves had to go.

O-U-G-H

(some thoughts, thowts, or thoots thereon)

This letter combination makes it tough
for people learning English. Who can bluff
his way, pronouncing *though, bough, cough,* and *sough*
as if, when he has finished, that's enough?

It isn't. He will find he's not quite *through*.
I'm glad we just spell *do* the way we do.
It might be *dough*. Why shouldn't *cough* be *coo?*
Sough's *suff*, but also *sow*. *Bough* might be *boo*.

Supposing *though*'s *not tho*, but more like *thoff*,
and *sough*'s *sow*'s not a pig that *sows*, but *soff?*
then pigs might eat from *truffs*, not from a *troff*.
and you'd mix cough-links up with cuffs that *coff*.

I bow to you; the bow-wow barks; a bow
shoots arrows, fixes ribbons. So we go,
since that pig's *trough* could very well be *trow*,
except that *trow*'s not just a rhyme for *flow:*

trow rhymes with *ow* as in an *Ouch!* I guess
that's all we'd better say about this mess.

Jamboree

A rhyme for ham? *Jam.*
A rhyme for mustard? *Custard.*
A rhyme for steak? *Cake.*
A rhyme for rice? *Another slice.*
A rhyme for stew? *You.*
A rhyme for mush? *Hush!*
A rhyme for prunes? *Goons.*
A rhyme for pie? *I.*
A rhyme for iced tea? *Me.*
For the pantry shelf? *Myself.*

Daybreak

Dawn? blinks Fawn.
What's going on?

Day! screams Jay:
Day, *Day* — Today!

That's so, caws Crow.
You didn't know?

Faint streak of light:
Check that, Bob White?

We see it: Squa-a-a-w-w-k!
(three Nighthawks talk).

Too loud, cries Cloud:
You boys too loud!

You want to wake
some sleepy Snake?

Or hear me sing?
chirps Chipperwing.

Amen to *that!*
squeaks Flit the Bat.

Amen to flittern,
too, booms Bittern.

I cease to prowl
at dawn, says Owl;

You mean you perch
on *me*, brags Birch.

In truth, in troth,
murmurmurs Moth

who likes it dark
in Birch's bark.

Sky's *really* grey
now. *Day!* screams Jay.

Yes. Take a look,
says Trout in Brook.

You see that Fly?
Well, so do I.

I'll leave this ring
where Swallows wing.

Day's night for Fox;
to heck with clocks!

All's night for Moles
like us in holes.

Me too! I surface,
though, says Shrew.

Get off my ground!
cracks Scamperound,

the Squirrel. *My* log!
pipes Lep, the Frog.

69

Crawl under, Bug,
with me — with Slug.

OK, says Tree:
not under me.

Not under *him?*
mocks Broken Limb,

that tough old Oak?
I'm glad I broke.

You used to toss
in wind, says Moss;

you're rotten wood
now — very good.

Don't leave *your* house,
I notice, Mouse!

He's scared of Cat,
whines Water Rat.

Who wouldn't be?
twits Phoebe. We

birds have a slew
of danger. You

folks hide at will;
we fly, sit still.

A lot of harm
there, round that farm;

not Cow, of course,
or Pig, or Horse;

but Cat and Shrike
and Hawk — suchlike.

The woods are best:
here's where we nest.

Peek in, now. *Hush!*
says Hermit Thrush.

No nest of mine,
pants Porcupine:

all woods are tough.
I've had enough.

Old noisy Quill:
Keep still! Keep still!

You! Silence now!
That Farmer's Cow?

Just sound of axe,
quacks Duck. Relax.

Drum . . . *Drum?* Just some
old Grouse's drum.

No! *No!* thumps Snow-
shoe Rabbit. *No!*

That's Silver Tongue:
Hot Dog! He's young.

But on the loose,
warns Wren. Vamoose!

Run, run! bangs Gun,
lest you be done.

Where? *Where?* grunts Bear,
who looks like Scare.

Here, answers Deer,
who leaps like Fear . . .

No, *no!* says Doe.
It can't be so . . .

on, on, with Fawn.
Why *must* it dawn?

Think! Think! No, slink
away like Mink.

Hide! Hide! some Groundhog
whistles. *Hide!*

O bunk! sniffs Skunk,
the one with spunk.

Mr. Mixup Tells a Story

Under the rabbit there, I saw a tree —
Well, you know what I mean.
His ears were green and leafy . . . you asked me
to *tell* you, didn't you, just what I'd seen?

Well, anyhow, out peered that big red box.
Red fox? Did I say *box?* A fox it was!
He didn't see me. I looked up my clocks . . .
My *watch?* My watch to watch how long he does.

How long he *took?* A nice word, *took.* That's right . . .
to spot my rabbit up above his spine —
his pine. No, rabbits don't have wings. It's quite
enough to wiggle nose. Can't wiggle mine.

Ten days went by. You say *ten minutes?* Why?
Because it happened yesterday? It should.
Then suddenly I saw the fellow fly.
Which fellow? Couldn't he? Oh, yes, he could.

And that old boxed-up wolf. I tell you he . . .
I don't know which direction. What's the diff?
He didn't catch — he wasn't after *me.*
What rabbit? Well, speak up! No matter if.

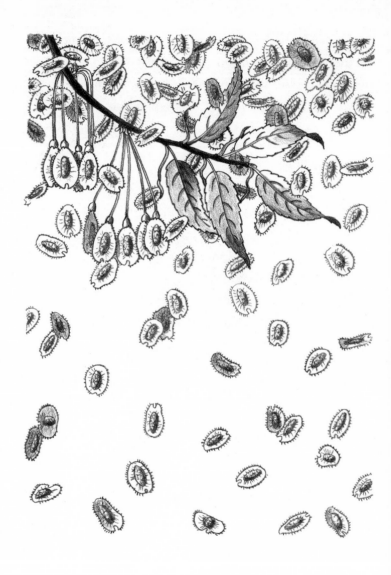

Elm Seed Blizzard

Along about then, the middle of May,
I say to myself: "any day . . ."
And I guess up there in the tall elm trees
The leaves say something like "Listen, breeze:
It's no good *whispering* stuff; just *blow!*
There's a skyful of seed here set to go."
And the breeze perks up
And the seeds fly loose —
Not hard like acorns, or cones like spruce —
But tiny saucers without a cup,
Till the air is full of their golden flutter
On street and sidewalk, lawn and gutter;
On windowsills, on doorsteps, mats;
On coats and pants and skirts and hats;
On people, dogs; in shoes, in cars;
On roller-skates, on handlebars;
On everything and everywhere;
Pale flakes of gold with piles to spare.

Well, a big wind comes and blows it all
Up down the street in a golden wall

To fill the air and fill your pockets
With billions out of a billion sockets:
Every saucer papery-thin:
One seed in the middle of each, sealed in.

If it happens to rain, then a cornflake slush,
Like a yellow boxtop cereal mush
Is under your feet, with a swirling flow
By the curbstone: squash, squash, squash, you go,
Till the cloggy mass that the sun dries out
Makes little gold islands all about.

You'd think, with all these seeds around,
A million elms would spring from the ground!
But nothing happens: the golden storm
Has gone like snow when the air gets warm:
Gone down the drain, gone up the sky,
Gone out with the cleaning trucks gone by —
Though somewhere, far away from me,
One lost blown seed becomes a tree.

Along about then, the middle of May,
I say to myself: "any day . . ."
I have only to say it. The trees let go,
And the air goes gold with a golden snow.

Trouble with Pies

Tomorrow's Christmas Day: three kinds of pies —
apple, mince, and pumpkin — all same size,
though not much bigger round than hungry eyes.

Since my first try at pie, I cannot choose
between mince, apple, pumpkin; or refuse
one, taking two of all those three good twos.

Apple and mince? Apple and pumpkin? What?
Leave pumpkin out, or mince? Well I guess not!
Pumpkin and mince? No apple have I got.

It would be better — best — to take all three;
but somehow that's not what they say to me.
"Which *do* you want?" they say. I say, "Let's see . . ."

Singular Indeed

One mouse adds up to many mice,
One louse adds up to lots of lice,
One chickenhouse to chickenhice.

The grouse — a noble bird! But *grice!*
What would you feed *them* — rouse or rice?
Or some old slouse of bread, or slice?

Take tub — you take it. Like to souse?
Or sice? One cold as ouse or ice
Is not so nouse, is not so nice.

Books Fall Open

Books fall open,
you fall in,
delighted where
you've never been;
hear voices not once
heard before,
reach world on world
through door on door;
find unexpected
keys to things
locked up beyond
imaginings.
What *might* you be,
perhaps *become*,
because one book
is somewhere? Some
wise delver into
wisdom, wit,
and wherewithal
has written it.

True books will venture,
dare you out,
whisper secrets,
maybe shout
across the gloom
to you in need,
who hanker for
a book to read.

Ivory

A cake of soap, a toothpick mast,
a paper sail, ahoy, avast,
and other sloopy sounds, and John
is in the bath with nothing on.

He wastes a lot of soap each tub
he takes, but he's not one to scrub;
and soapboats do the sudsing while
the boy is sailing up the Nile.

The White Nile's full of *sudd* — a word
(two d's) of which too few have heard:
some vegetable stuff that floats
and fills the river, stops the boats

from running up and down at will.
But John's boat isn't all that still.
His only problem, ever since
he made a boat, is when to rinse.

Knotholes

To make a knothole,
Knock out the knot;
And having a knothole,
What have you got?
You've got whatever
The fence shut in.
With lots of knots,
Where they have been
You've got whatever
The fence shut out.
You see what knotholes
Are all about?

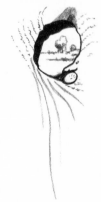

November Bares the Robin's Nest

November bares the robin's nest
We had to part the leaves to see;
And even then we thought it best
To glance and go, and let it be.
The mother in another tree
Said "Don't you dare to touch those eggs!"
We never did. They hatched, and we
Thought: *What big mouths and what small legs.*

The fledglings fattened, feathered out;
The days grew long, mouths widened wide.
I guess the worms and bugs about
All vanished from the countryside.
How well the full green leaves could hide
Such dark digestion going on!
But then one day the youngsters tried
Their wings. Three days, and they were gone.

Bone-dry, the vacant nest shows up —
A shabby, tattered thing of straw
And stuff, so little like the cup
Of skyblue eggs that first we saw.
The rains have rotted it; the raw
Damp easterly has torn and frayed
The edges. On the branch, *caw-caw*,
The black crow settles and is swayed.

Wintry

Hylas in the spring,
Crickets in the fall:
In winter not a thing
To sing itself at all.

Fireflies follow May,
Bonfires Halloween;
Nothing lights up grey
Old winter in between.

Come Christmas

You see this Christmas tree all silver gold?
It stood out many winters in the cold,

with tinsel sometimes made of crystal ice,
say once a winter morning — maybe twice.

More often it was trimmed by fallen snow
so heavy that the branches bent, with no

one anywhere to see how wondrous is
the hand of God in that white world of his.

And if you think it lonely through the night
when Christmas trees in houses take the light,

remember how his hand put up one star
in this same sky so long ago afar.

All stars are hung so every Christmas tree
has one above it. Let's go out and see.

Forget It

I'm not too sure that all I've read
Is under my hat or over my head;
What I've forgotten, so far as I see,
Is a matter between myself and me.
If things remembered since I was young
I don't keep right on the tip of my tongue,
It doesn't mean *something* won't come out!
What is it you want to know about?

Orion

Orion in the cold December sky
Looks out upon the earth, the leaves gone by,
Swings over church and steeple down the slack
Of starfields to the western gate out back.
I see his belt (three stars) the studding grace
Of giants striding up through stellar space
Indifferent to satellites and all
That man has made and rocketed. How tall
He stands! How glad I am to know
His name and shape. One wonders here, below
His range and region, why we do not dare
In sight of all the bounty earth can bear,
In loneliness of flesh and blood and bone,
To walk as steadfast, and to walk alone.

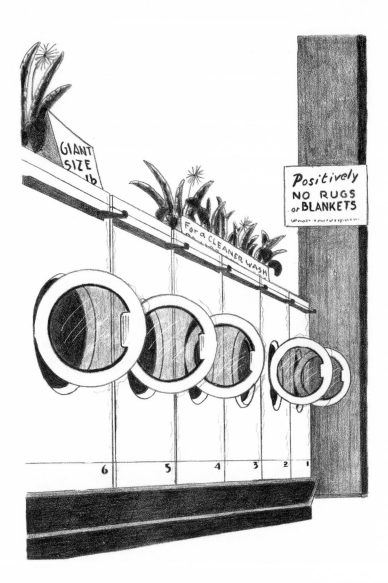

Laundromat

You'll find me in the Laundromat — just me and shirts and stuff:
Pajamas, pillowcases, socks and handkerchiefs enough.
I've put them in my special tub — the third one from the right,
And set the switch for *Warm*, and shoved the coin and got the light,
And sprinkled blue detergent on the water pouring in,
Closed down the lid and bought a Coke to watch the shakes begin
To travel up the line of empty units. How they show
Their pleasure just to feel one fellow full and on the go!
Well, now it's all one train: a nice long rumbly kind of freight,
Of which I am the engineer. We're running on the straight.
In Diesel Number Three I've got the throttle open wide,
And blow for every crossing through the pleasant countryside.
The light turns amber. Pretty soon some other washers bring
Their bulgy bags of clothes and make tubs nine and seven sing.
But nine and seven haven't got the squiggle, squash, and drive
Of Number Three. May sound alike to you, but I'm alive
To certain water music that the third one seems to make.
I hear it change from rinse to spin, and now it doesn't shake.
Green Light! The spin is over, the longer job is done;
And what was washed is plastered to the walls from being spun.
You'd think the tub is empty, since the bottom's clear and bright;
I'm glad the spinning earth can't throw *us* out into the night!

For that is where we'd go, because the sky is not a wall;
But earth's content to hold us with our dirty shirts and all.
Still, spinning *is* a funny thing: the tub goes like a top.
The dryer, on the other hand, runs like a wheel. I plop
The damp unsorted pillowcases, hanks, and socks, and what
Into a kind of squirrel cage that generates a lot
Of heat when set at *Medium*. But this one needs the dime
I haven't got! I'll dry some other clothes some other time.

First and Last

A tadpole hasn't a pole at all,
And he *doesn't* live in a hole in the wall.

You've got it wrong: a polecat's not
A cat on a pole. And I'll tell you what:

A bullfrog's never a bull; and how
Could a cowbird possibly be a cow?

A kingbird, though, *is* a kind of king,
And he chases a crow like anything.

Snowflakes

Sometime this winter if you go
To walk in soft new-falling snow
When flakes are big and come down slow

To settle on your sleeve as bright
As stars that couldn't wait for night,
You won't know what you have in sight —

Another world — unless you bring
A magnifying glass. This thing
We call a snowflake is the king

Of crystals. Do you like surprise?
Examine him three times his size:
At first you won't believe your eyes.

Stars look alike, but flakes do not:
No two the same in all the lot
That you will get in any spot

You chance to be, for every one
Come spinning through the sky has none
But his own window-wings of sun:

Joints, points, and crosses. What could make
Such lacework with no crack or break?
In billion billions, no mistake?

Answering Your Question

In grapes I know there *may* be seeds;
In prunes I know there will be.
My name is Shadwell Presswood Leeds,
My sister's name is Trilby.

The Doctor

When the doctor comes
he always hums
Ta-dee, ta-diddle-doo;
which means a lot —
"Well, what have you got?"
"Hello!" or "How are *you?*"

His bag is black,
I'm on my back.
Ta-dee, ta-diddle-o:
His stethoscope
will get the dope
on how things are below.

He hums his "Young
man, how's that tongue?"
Ta-dee, ta-diddle-dee:
I stick it out.
His hum's about
like language now to me.

With a snappy shake
(don't thermometers break?)
Ta-dee, ta-diddle-die:
he sticks it in
as I try to grin;
but he hums "Be quiet!" My,

what a hum-drum hum
if results are bum,
what tiddles and tas if slick.
Humming under his breath,
is he scared to death
of mumps? The hum goes quick

to a fast pulse. Oh,
but it idles slow
while fingers probe the jaw
for glands just not
I forget just what.
The throat? "Say ah-h-h, not *aw-w-w!*"

breaks *dee-diddle-doo*
right smack in two;

and he generally adds "Now, rest!"
when he goes. When he's gone,
though, his hum hangs on
in the stuff in the medicine chest.

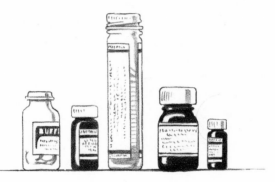

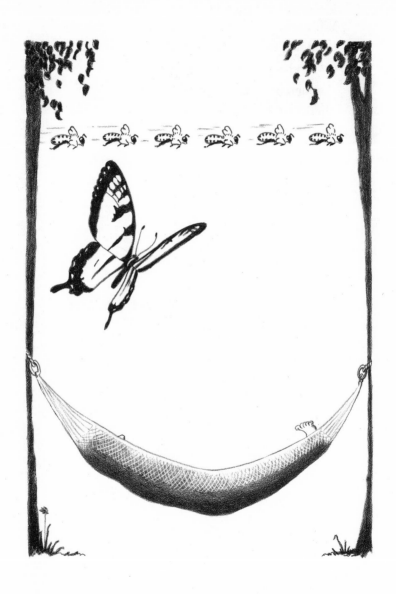

Hammock

Our hammock swings between two trees,
So when the garden's full of bees,
And if the hammock's full of me,
They fly right over, bee by bee.
They fly goshawful fast and straight —
I guess a bee is never late;
And if I can't quite see the line,
I try to think I hear the whine:
Much higher than the drowsy sound
Of having hives of bees around.
Provided bees don't bother me,
I'm glad to let a bee just be.
Some day I'll put a microphone
Inside their door and pipe the drone

Above my hammock, fall asleep
To bees all busy-buzz that keep
Their distance. Meanwhile here I lie.
I'm watching now a butterfly,
Unhurried, knowing not what's up:
A daisy, rose, or buttercup?
Not caring where he's been, or where
He's flapping to. He fills the air
With little flags and floats away
As I do on this summer's day.